A Smidgen for a Pigeon

Author and Illustrator:
Alexandra Michelle Hobson

ISBN: 1468123386
ISBN-13: 9781468123388
Library of Congress Control Number: 2011963370
CreateSpace, North Charleston, SC

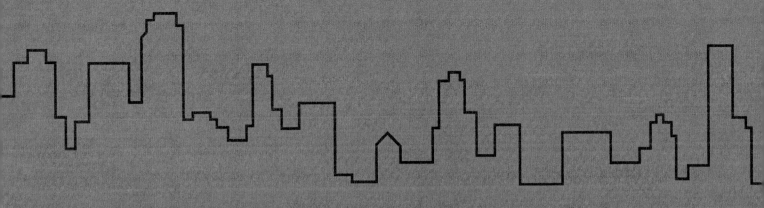

DEDICATION PAGE

I'd like to dedicate this book to my siblings; RJ & Jordan
and to my awesome cousins, Jack, Kate, Mike, Eric,
Annie, Gage, Jaden, Colin, and Kiera.

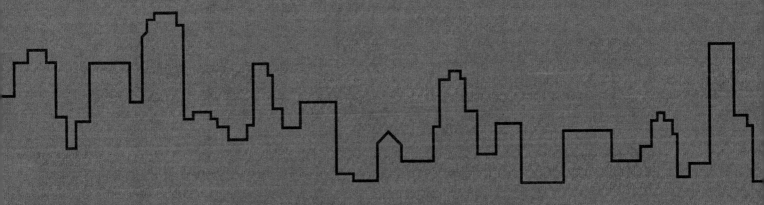

ACKNOWLEDGEMENTS

A big thanks to my mom and dad for supporting me all these years and encouraging me to do what I love.

A special thanks to my favorite instructor, Kim Parr. You were patient with me and guided me through the whole process of creating this book.

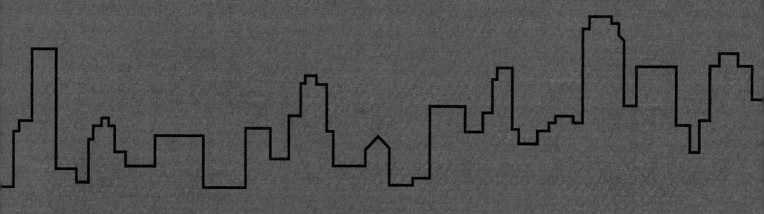

In the crowded location of Baltimore City,

Where you rarely see a stray dog or a mangy kitty.

But what you will see in this bustling place,

Are flocks of pigeons, often called a disgrace.

This story is to change that; no, this isn't a trick.

The tale of a humble pigeon, with his wife and his chick.

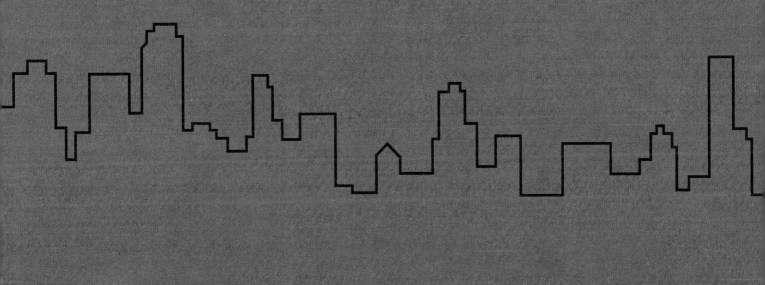

3

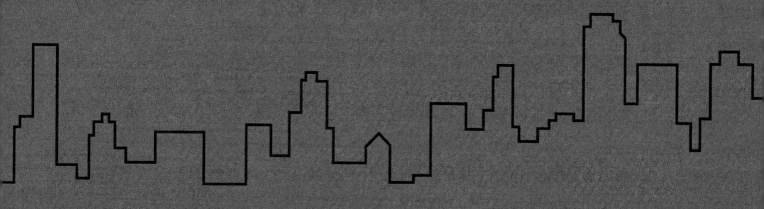

His name is Ray; a hardworking bird.

To say he's a disgrace is completely absurd.

He works long hours for his boss named Jim.

He finds treasures on the streets, and brings them to him.

If he did well, he would soon be full of glee.

Some food for his wife, Kate, and his little chick, Bee.

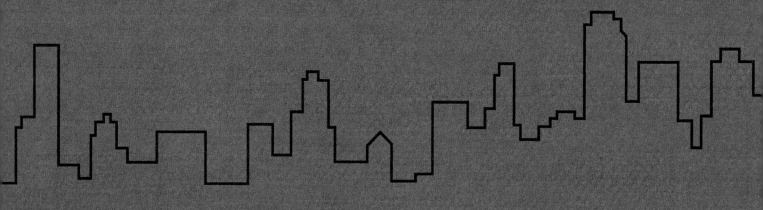

But if he did bad, I am sad to say,

His plea for a meal would be turned away.

His family never complained, despite not being fed.

Kate would say, "We weren't hungry anyways. Now Bee,

time for bed."

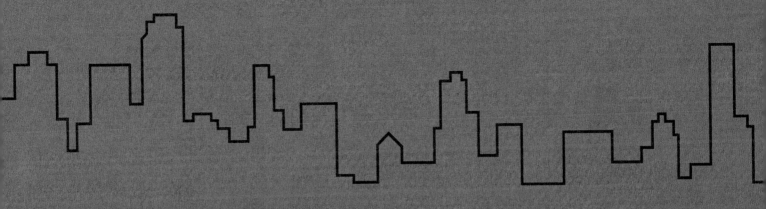

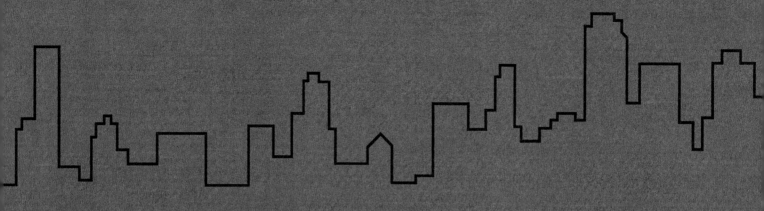

Ray sunk his head, feeling helpless and full of sorrow.

He vowed to himself, he would do twice as good tomorrow.

Ray's job is dangerous, being around humans all the time.

Once, he was kicked real hard for picking up

someone's lost dime.

He didn't bother people, he went elsewhere to poo.

But people still hated him, and spit on him too!

9

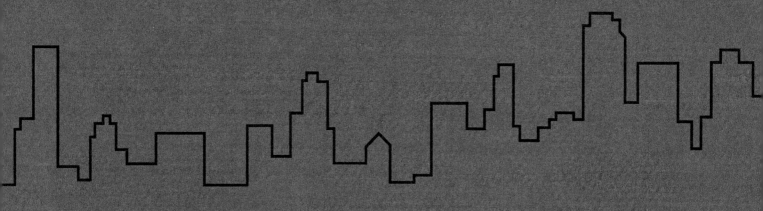

He wished for his neighbor's job, a carrier pigeon named Rob.
All he had to do is fly somewhere, and he would get
corn on the cob.
Rob lived in a wooden house, that someone built for him.
While Ray got kicked by humans, and got bread crumbs
from Jim.
But he couldn't be a carrier pigeon, all the jobs were taken.
Jim would be furious, if he knew Ray was flakin'.

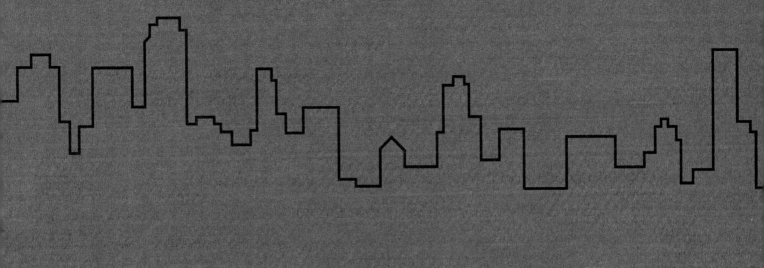

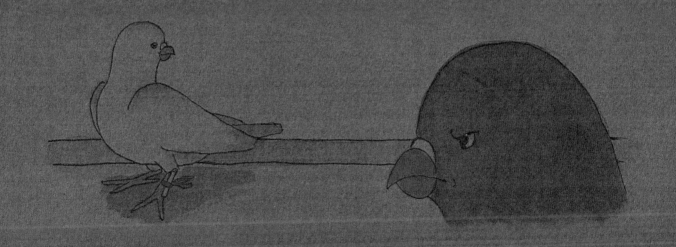

11

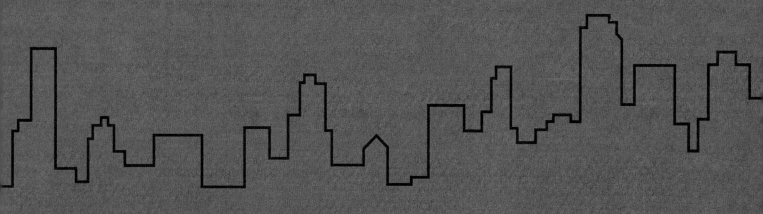

"I don't understand!" Ray said "I'm just like a dove!
I'm seen as a rat with wings, but they're angels from above?"
"The colors of my feathers, " Ray said, "What a shame."
So, he was born grey and black, is he to blame?
Why can't people see past the dull colors of black
and grey?

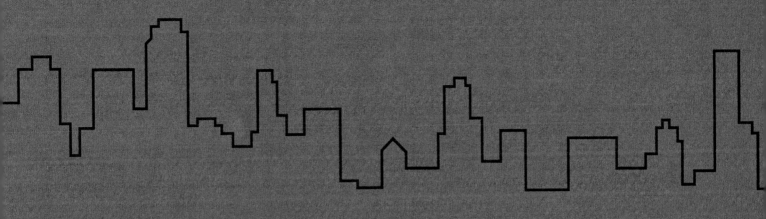

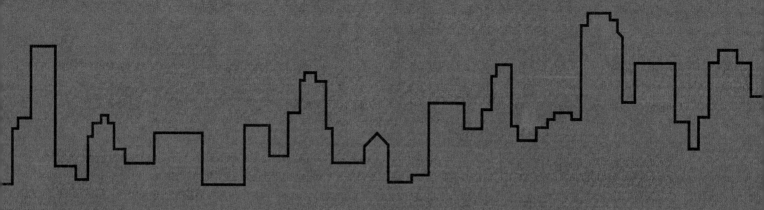

Then he thought a bit, thought about his life.

Was all of this stress really worth the strife?

He could fly away, no worries anymore!

He got excited and jumped off the floor!

Ray was ready to go, he was ready to fly!

He felt a tug on his tail, and heard a small cry.

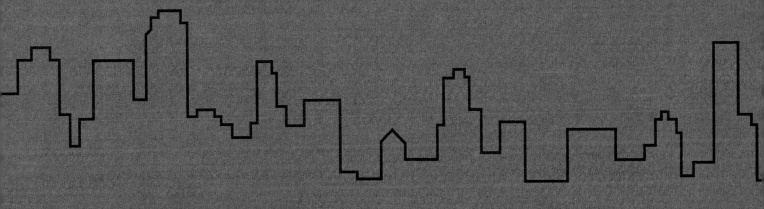

15

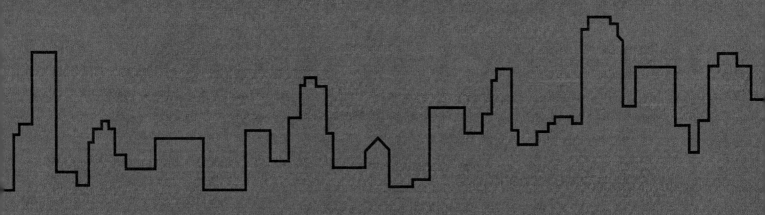

He turned around and saw his precious Bee.

She exclaimed, "Daddy, please! Don't leave me!"

He stopped in his tracks, and looked in her eyes,

He remembered why he works so hard, why he even tries.

No matter how much he hurt, if nothing got better,

Losing Kate and Bee would be the worst thing ever.

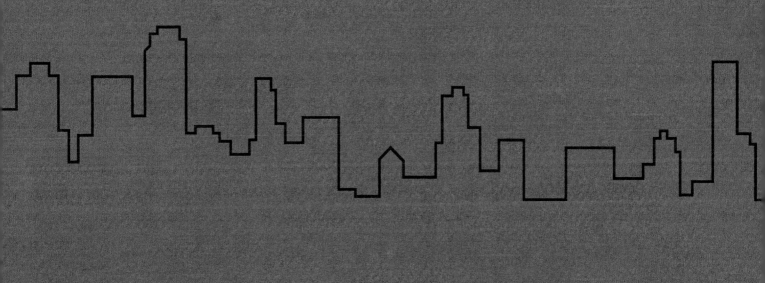

17

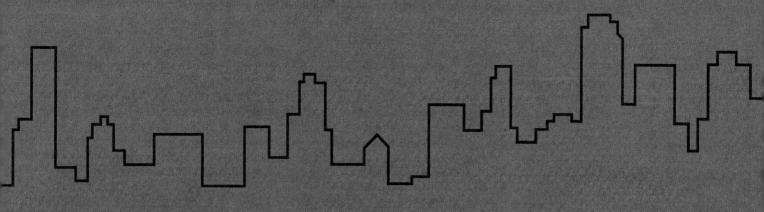

From that moment on, even when put to the test,

Ray always tried to do his absolute best.

If he ever failed, well, he never really did...

How can you fail with a great wife and great kid?

He would endure anything for them, even a horrid

human being.

This is because without love, life isn't worth seeing.

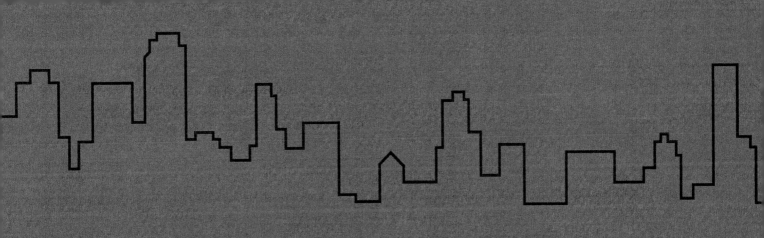

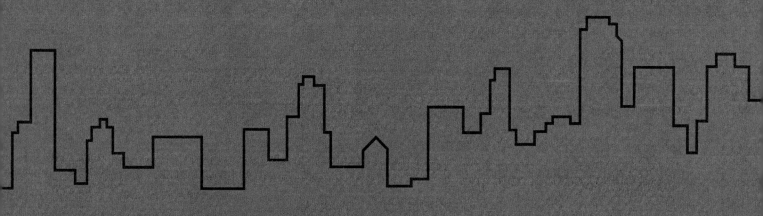

So, next time you see a pigeon, color dull as lead,

Ask him how he's doing instead of kicking him in the head.

Because maybe, just maybe, he has a family just like you.

You don't see him comin' round and smacking you with a shoe.

When it comes down to it, just keep giving.

Because if you're not giving love, you're not living.

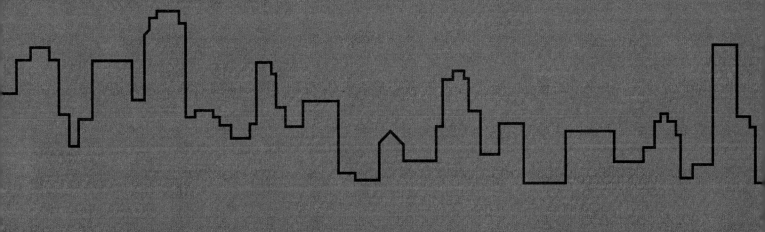

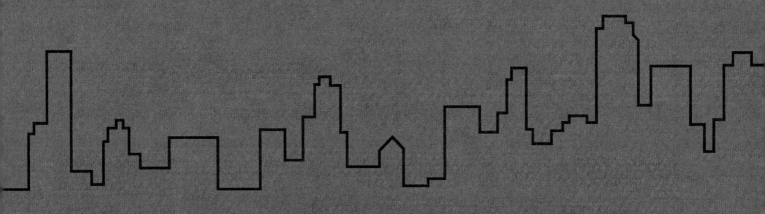

ABOUT THE AUTHOR

Alexandra knew at an early age that she loved exploring many different mediums of art. Only a senior in high school, she wrote and illustrated this book; her very first children's book.

46413290R00015